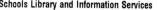

The Wild Swans

Hans Christian Andersen

Translated by Naomi Lewis

Illustrated by Anne Yvonne Gilbert

Barefoot Books
Celebrating Art and Story

Introduction

Hans Christian Andersen (1805–1875) was born on 2 April, in Odense, Denmark. His mother was a peasant — hard working, pious and illiterate. His father was a shoemaker by trade, but by nature a scholarly man of advanced ideas. Poverty made him leave for the wars when his son was only six, but before then he had told the child that every non-human *thing* — a leaf, a toy, a darning needle — has its own story. He had also taught him how to make and work a toy theatre. Both 'gifts' were to be invaluable to Andersen the writer.

At fourteen, young Andersen set out for Copenhagen. After three cold and hungry years of knocking at doors, scribbling plays and haunting the theatre, he was at last given a formidable guardian — but had to endure a grim (and pointless) school 'education'. Once free, he fast became known in Denmark for his poems, fiction and travel pieces. Yet his true gift would surface in 1835, with a booklet of four tales told in a new way. More followed. As soon as they were translated, leading writers of each country hailed him as

Master. And so 'the washerwoman's crazy son', as the neighbours called him, became the best known, most loved Dane in the entire reading — and listening — world.

The Wild Swans appeared in 1837, one of the tales that first made Andersen's name. Unlike most of his stories, it drew its plot from older sources (chiefly Grimm), yet no one else could have written the version that we know. What is special here is the thrill of the great descriptive scenes: the night in the summer wood, the furious sea in storm, the eerie midnight churchyard and the marvellous journey through the clouds. Andersen lived in a time of invention and change, the stagecoach giving way to the train, the sailing vessel to the steamship. These held particular significance for him, as he was a tireless traveller. But aerial flight, which he longed for, was still in the future. No matter. Imagination at its most magical makes the sky journey in this tale.

Naomi Lewis

Far, far away, in the land where the swallows fly during our winter, there lived a king who had eleven sons and one daughter, Elisa. The eleven brothers — princes all of them — went to school, each wearing a star at his heart and a sword at his side. They wrote on gold slates with diamond pencils; whatever they read, they learnt at once. You could tell straight off that they were princes! Their sister Elisa sat on a little stool made of looking-glass, and had a picture book that cost half a kingdom.

Oh, they lived royally, those children! But it did not last. The king, their father, married an evil queen, and she didn't care for the children at all. They realised this on the very first day. A great celebration was held to welcome her, and the children, too, decided to play at guests-for-tea. But instead of cakes and roasted apples, which they were usually given, the queen allowed them only a cupful of sand. They would have to pretend that it was cakes and apples, she told them.

A week later she sent off little Elisa into the country, to live with a peasant family. And it wasn't long before she had filled the king's head with such shocking tales about the poor young princes that he wished to have nothing more to do with them.

'Out you go!' said the wicked queen to the boys. 'Fend for yourselves as you may. Fly off as voiceless birds!'

Yet she could not do as much harm as she wished, for they turned into eleven beautiful wild swans. With a strange cry, they flew out of the palace windows, over the fields and forests, far away.

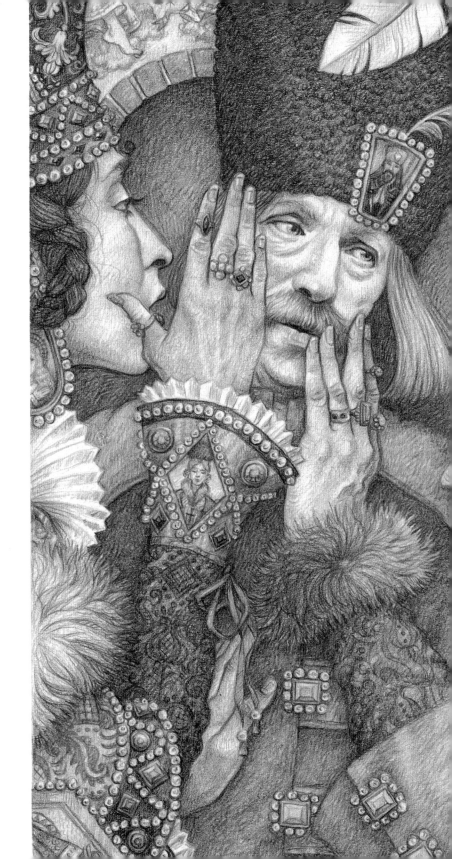

Early next morning they passed the place where their sister Elisa had been sent. They circled about the cottage roof, flapping their wings and craning their necks. But nobody heard or saw. At last they had to fly on, upwards into the clouds, out into the wide world.

Poor little Elisa sat in the cottage playing with a green leaf, the only toy she had. She pricked a hole in it and peeped through at the sun. The brightness seemed like the bright eyes of her brothers.

Time passed, one day just like another. But whenever the wind blew through the garden, it whispered to the roses, 'Could anyone be more beautiful than you?'

And the roses would answer, 'Yes — Elisa is more beautiful.'

What they said was the truth.

When Elisa was fifteen she was brought back to the palace. The evil queen, seeing how beautiful she was, was very vexed indeed. She would have promptly turned Elisa into another wild swan like her brothers, but she did not dare just yet, for the king had asked to see his daughter.

Early the next morning, the queen went into the bathroom with three toads. She kissed the first and said, 'Hop on to Elisa's head, and make her as slow and dull as you.' Kissing the second, she said, 'Make her look just like you, so that her father will not know her.' Then she kissed the third toad, whispering, 'Fill her with evil, so that she knows no peace.' She put the toads into the clear water, which at once took on a strange greenish tinge. Yet Elisa seemed not to notice them. And when she rose from the water, they were gone — but three scarlet poppies were floating there. If the toads had not been poisoned by the kiss of the wicked queen, they would have become red roses. But flowers they had become from Elisa's touch alone.

When the queen perceived how she had failed, she rubbed Elisa's skin with dark brown walnut juice and made her hair look wild and tangled. You wouldn't have recognised her!

And so, when her father saw her, he was shocked.

'That is not my daughter!' he declared.

No one else at court would have anything to do with her, except the watchdog and the swallows, and who ever bothered about what *they* thought?

Poor Elisa started to cry. She crept out of the palace, and walked all day through field and moor and meadow, until she reached a great dark forest, leading to the sea. She had no idea where she was but she fixed her mind on her brothers. They had been driven forth like herself, and now she would go to the ends of the earth to find them.

Night fell, and she lay down on the moss. All was silent; the air was mild and touched with a greenish light — it came from hundreds of glow-worms. There were so many that when she gently touched a branch, a falling shower of sparkling creatures lit the dark like stars.

All that night she dreamt about her brothers. They were playing together as they did when they were children, writing with the diamond pencils on the gold slates, looking at the beautiful picture book that was worth half a kingdom. Only now they were setting down all that had befallen them, bold deeds and strange adventures. Everything in the picture book seemed to come alive; the birds sang, the people stepped out of the pages and spoke to her. But when she turned over a page they jumped straight back, so as not to get into the wrong picture.

When she awoke the sun was high overhead, though she could hardly see through the thick leaves and branches of the trees. But where the sunbeams shimmered through the moving leaves there was a dancing golden haze. The air was filled with the smell of fresh green grass; the birds flew so near that they seemed about to perch on her shoulder. She heard the splashing of water; it came from a spring which flowed into a pool, so clear that you could see the sandy bed below.

But when Elisa saw her own face in the water, she was startled — it was so grimy and strange. She dipped her hand into the pool and rubbed her eyes and forehead — what a contrast! Her own clear skin shone through.

She took off her clothes and stepped into the
fresh cool water — and a more beautiful
princess could not have been found anywhere
in the world.

As she set off again, she met an old woman,
who gave her some berries from a basket that
she was carrying. Elisa asked her if she had
come across eleven princes riding through the
forest.

'No,' said the old woman. 'But yesterday I
saw eleven swans with golden crowns on
their heads swimming down yonder river.'
Elisa thanked her and walked along the
winding water until it reached the sea. There
the great ocean lay before her. What was she
to do?

Then she saw, scattered about the sea grass, one, two, three, four — eleven swans' feathers. The sun had almost set. She looked up; eleven swans were flying towards the land, like a long white ribbon. Each had a golden crown on its head. Flapping their great wings, they landed near her.

At that moment the sun sank below the water; the swans seemed to shed their feathery covering — and there stood eleven handsome princes. Elisa ran forward and threw herself into their arms, calling them each by name. They, in turn, were overjoyed to see their little sister, and they told her their strange tale.

'We brothers,' said the oldest, 'have to fly as swans so long as the sun is in the sky. When night has come we return to human shape; that is why we must look for a landing place well before sunset. If we were flying high in the air when darkness came, we should hurtle down as humans to our deaths.

'We do not dwell here any more. Our home is now a land far across the sea. To reach it we have to cross the vast ocean — and there is no island where we can rest in our human form during the night. Only one thing saves us. About halfway across, a little rock rises out of the water — just large enough to hold us standing close together. If it were not there we would never be able to visit our native land again, since we need the two longest days of the year for our flight. Once a year we fly over this mighty forest, and gaze at the palace where we were born, and circle over the tower of the church where our mother is buried.

'The wild horses gallop across the plains as they did in our childhood; the charcoal burner still sings the old songs that we danced to as children. Here is our native ground, the place that will always draw us back. But tomorrow we must set off again for that other land, and we cannot return for another year. Have you the courage to come with us, little sister?'

'Oh, take me with you,' Elisa said.

All that night they set about weaving a net of willow bark and rushes. When the sun rose and the brothers turned into swans, they picked up the net with their beaks, and flew with Elisa into the clouds. But the youngest hovered just overhead to shade her with his wings from the sun's hot rays.

Now they had reached such a height that the first ship they saw looked like a white seagull resting on the waves. A great cloud lay behind them, a mountain of cloud, and on it Elisa saw the shadows of herself and her brothers. They were like giants' shadows, vast and wonderful. But the sun rose higher and cloud and shadow pictures disappeared.

All the long day they flew, like arrows in the sky. Yet, swift as they were, they were slower than at other times, for they now had their sister to carry. Night was near, the air was full of thunder, but there was still no sign of the tiny rock. Elisa looked down with terror. At any moment now her brothers would change to humans and all would fall to their deaths.

Black clouds surrounded them; storm winds churned the leaden water; flash after flash of lightning pierced the gloom.

Suddenly, the birds headed downwards. The sun was already halfway into the sea — but now, for the first time, she saw the little rock; it could have been a seal's head looking out of the water. Then her feet touched the ground, and at that moment the sun went out like the last spark on a piece of burning paper. All round her stood her brothers, human now, sheltering her from the dashing waves.

At dawn the air was clear and still. The sun rose; the eleven swans soared from their rock, with Elisa on her airy raft, and went on with their journey. From far above, the white foam on the dark green waves looked like thousands of floating swans.

Then Elisa looked ahead, and beheld a range of mountains, with glittering icy peaks. In their midst was a mighty palace, at least a mile in length. Below were groves of waving palm trees, and wonderful flowers, vast in size, like millwheels. Yet all this seemed suspended in the air. Was it the land they were making for? But when she asked, the swans shook their heads. What she was seeing, they told her, was the cloud palace of the fairy Morgana, lovely but ever changing; no mortal might enter there.

And as Elisa gazed, mountains, palace, trees and flowers all dissolved, and in their place rose a score of noble churches, with lofty towers. She thought that she heard organ music — or was it the sound of the sea? Then, when they seemed quite near, the churches changed to a fleet of ships sailing just below. She looked again — there were no ships; all she saw was a whirl of mist over the water. Sea and air and sky are ever in motion, ever changing; no vision comes to the watcher twice.

And then Elisa glimpsed land at last. Blue mountains of rare beauty rose up before her; she could just discern forests of cedar, cities and palaces. The swans came down, and Elisa found herself at the mouth of a hillside cave; an opening almost hidden by a web of vines and other delicate greenery.

'You can sleep here safely,' the youngest brother said.

Was it a dream? She thought that she was flying through the air, straight to the cloud castle of the fairy Morgana. The fairy herself came to meet her. She was radiant and beautiful — but she was also very much like the old woman who had given her berries in the forest, and had told her of the swans with golden crowns.

'Your brothers can be freed,' said the fairy.

'But it will take no ordinary courage. Look at this stinging nettle. It grows plentifully round the cave where you are now sleeping — and in only one other place: on churchyard graves. Now, first you must gather them yourself, though they will sting and burn your skin. Then you must tread on them with bare feet until they are like flax. This you must twist into thread and weave into cloth; from that cloth you must make eleven shirts like coats of mail with sleeves. Throw one of these over each of your brothers and the spell will break. But — this is important — until you finish your task, even if it takes years, you must not speak. A single word will pierce your brothers' hearts like a knife. Their lives depend on your silence. Remember!'

She touched Elisa's hand with the nettle. It scorched her skin like fire, and she awoke. It was bright daylight; nearby lay a nettle like the one she had seen in her dream. Elisa went outside the cave — yes, there the nettles were! She would start at once. She plucked an armful, trampled them with bare feet, and began to twist the green flax into thread.

At sunset her brothers returned. At first her silence alarmed them. But then they guessed that she must be doing this strange work for their sakes.

All that night she worked. When day returned, the swan-brothers flew far afield, and she sat alone, but never did time go so fast. One shirt was already finished, and she started on the next.

All at once, a sound rang through the mountains — the sound of a distant hunting horn. She heard the barking of dogs and she was seized with terror.

Then a great hound sprang out of the bushes. It was followed at once by another, then another; they made for the mouth of the cave. Before many minutes, all the huntsmen had gathered at her hiding place, and the most handsome of all stepped forward. He was the king of that land. He saw Elisa, and she seemed to him the most beautiful girl in the world.

'How do you come to be here?' he asked.

Elisa shook her head; she dared not speak.

'Come with me,' said the king. 'If you are as good as you are beautiful, you shall wear a gold crown on your head, and the finest of my castles shall be your home.'

He lifted her on to his horse and they galloped off through the mountains. His companions rode behind.

It was day's end before they reached the royal city. The king led Elisa into his palace, where sparkling fountains splashed into marble pools and the lofty walls and ceilings were covered with marvellous paintings. But she wept and grieved and saw nothing. Listless and pale, she let the women dress her in royal robes, twine her hair with pearls and cover her damaged hands with gloves.

Then at last she entered the great hall. She was so dazzlingly beautiful that all the court bowed low before her and the king announced that she would be his bride. But the archbishop shook his head and whispered that the wood maiden from the forest must surely be a sorceress who had cast a spell on his heart.

Yet the king would not hear a word against her. He ordered the music to strike up and the rarest dishes to be served; she was taken through fragrant gardens and splendid halls. But nothing touched her grief.

Then the king showed her a little room which would be her own. Carpeted in green, hung with costly green tapestries, it was made to look like the cave where she had been found. On the floor lay the bundle of nettles and flax; from the ceiling hung the one shirt that she had finished. A huntsman had brought these things along as a curiosity.

'Here you can dream yourself back in your old home,' said the king. 'Now, when you wish, you can amuse yourself by thinking of that bygone time.'

When Elisa saw what was so near to her heart, a smile came to her lips, colour returned to her face and she kissed the king's hand. He took her in his arms and gave commands for all the church bells to be rung for their wedding. The lovely mute girl from the forest would be queen.

Then came the wedding day. The archbishop himself had to place the crown on Elisa's head, and he pressed it down so spitefully that it hurt. But she felt a deep affection for the good and handsome king, and day by day she loved him more and more. If only she could speak! But first, she had to complete her task. So each night, as the king slept, she would steal from his side, and go to her work in the room like a green cave. Six shirts were now complete. But she had no more flax. And only in the churchyard could she find the right nettles.

So at midnight, full of fear, she crept down through the moonlit garden, along the great avenues, and out into the lonely street that led to the churchyard. What a sight met her eyes! A ring of lamias, those witches that are half snake, half woman, sat round the largest gravestone. Elisa had to pass close by them, and they fastened their dreadful gaze upon her; but she prayed for safety, gathered the nettles and carried them back to the palace.

But not unnoticed. One person had seen and followed her — the archbishop. So his suspicions were true! The new queen *was* a witch.

In the church, after the service, he told all this to the king. The carved saints shook their heads as if to say: 'It is not so! Elisa is innocent!' But the archbishop chose to take this differently; the saints were shaking their heads at her sins.

Two heavy tears rolled down the king's face, and he went home with a troubled heart. He pretended to sleep at night, but no sleep came. Now, day by day, he grew more wretched. This troubled Elisa sorely, and added to her grief about her brothers. Her tears ran down on her royal velvet bodice and lay there like diamonds; but people saw only her beauty and her rich attire and wished that *they* were queen.

Still, her task was nearly done, for only a single shirt remained to be made. The trouble was that again she had no more flax, not a single nettle.

Once more she would have to go to the churchyard. She thought fearfully of the lonely midnight journey; but then she thought of her brothers.

She went — and the king and the archbishop followed her. They saw her disappear through the iron gates of the churchyard; they saw the frightful lamias on the graves. The king turned away in grief, for he thought that she had come to seek the company of these monsters — his own Elisa, his queen.

'The people shall judge her!' he said. And this the people did. They proclaimed her guilty, and ordered her to be burnt at the stake.

She was taken from the splendour of the palace and pushed into a dungeon, damp and dark. Instead of silken sheets and velvet pillows, the nettles and nettle-work cloth from her room had been tossed in, but she could have asked for no better gift. While boys outside sang jeering songs — 'The witch! The witch!' — she began to work on the last of the shirts.

The archbishop had arranged to spend the final hours in prayer with her, but when he came Elisa shook her head and pointed to the door. Her work must be finished that night. The archbishop went away, muttering angry words.

Poor Elisa! If only she could speak. Little mice ran over the floor; they dragged the nettles towards her, doing all that they could to help. A thrush sang all night through at the bars to give her hope.

At first light, it was still an hour before sunrise, the eleven brothers, in human form, stood at the castle gate and demanded to see the king. 'Impossible!' they were told. 'His majesty is asleep and cannot be disturbed.' They begged and pleaded; they threatened; the guard came down to see what the noise was about and at last the king appeared.

At that very moment the sun rose. Where were the eleven young men? Nowhere. But over the palace flew eleven wild swans.

From earliest daylight, crowds of people had jostled through the city gates; they all wanted to see the burning of the witch. There she was, in a cart dragged along by a forlorn old horse. She was wearing a smock made from coarse sacking; her lovely hair hung loose about her shoulders; her face was deathly pale, but her fingers never stopped working at the last of the green nettle shirts. The other ten lay at her feet.

The noisy mob still mocked and screeched:

'Look at the witch!' they yelled. 'See what she's up to! Still at her filthy witchcraft! Get it away from her! Tear it into a thousand pieces.'

They surged forward, and were just about to destroy her precious handiwork when down flew eleven great white swans. Beating their wings, they settled on the cart. The mob drew back in fear.

'It's a sign from heaven,' some of them whispered. 'She must be innocent.'

The executioner seized her hand — but she quickly flung the eleven garments over the swans. In their place were eleven handsome princes. Only the youngest had a swan's wing instead of an arm, because Elisa had had no time to finish the last sleeve.

'Now I may speak,' she said. 'I am no witch. I am innocent.'

The people hung their heads and kneeled before her.

'Yes, indeed she is innocent,' said the eldest brother. And he began to tell their long, strange story. As he spoke, a fragrance as from millions of roses filled the air; every piece of wood in the stake had taken root and put forth branches. There stood a mighty bush of the loveliest red roses. High at the summit was a single white flower, shining like a star. The king reached up and plucked it and laid it on Elisa's heart.

Then all the church bells rang of their own accord, and great flocks of birds flew overhead. And so began the journey back to the palace. A more joyful and radiant procession no king has ever yet seen.

To my parents, with love and affection — A. Y. G.

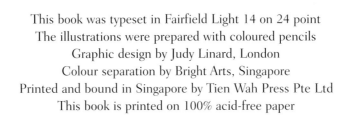

Barefoot Books
124 Walcot Street
Bath
BA1 5BG

This book was typeset in Fairfield Light 14 on 24 point
The illustrations were prepared with coloured pencils
Graphic design by Judy Linard, London
Colour separation by Bright Arts, Singapore
Printed and bound in Singapore by Tien Wah Press Pte Ltd
This book is printed on 100% acid-free paper

Hardcover ISBN 1-84148-118-1

British Cataloguing-in-Publication Data:
a catalogue record for this book is available from the British Library

1 3 5 7 9 8 6 4 2

At Barefoot Books, we celebrate art and story with books that open the
hearts and minds of children from all walks of life, inspiring them to
read deeper, search further, and explore their own creative gifts.
Taking our inspiration from many different cultures, we focus on
themes that encourage independence of spirit, enthusiasm for learning,
and acceptance of other traditions. Thoughtfully prepared by writers,
artists, and storytellers from all over the world, our products combine
the best of the present with the best of the past to educate our
children as the caretakers of tomorrow.

www.barefootbooks.com